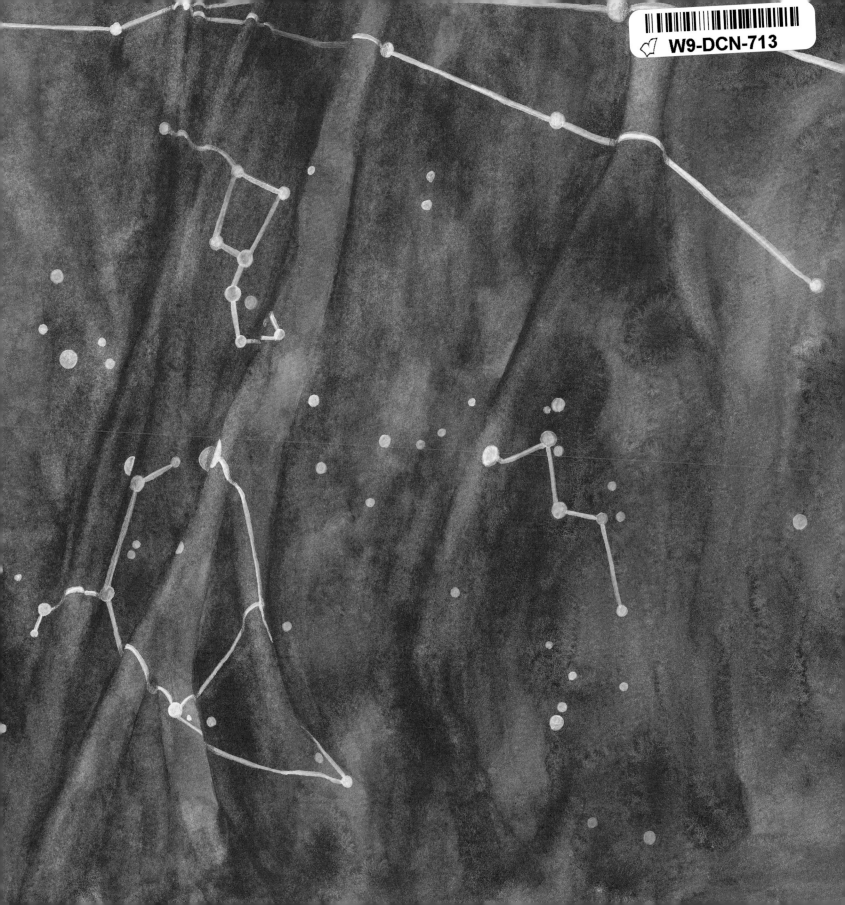

WHEN I WAKE UP

BY **SETH FISHMAN**

ILLUSTRATIONS BY **JESSIXA BAGLEY**

GREENWILLOW BOOKS, AN IMPRINT OF HARPERCOLLINSPUBLISHERS

Library of Congress Cataloging-in-Publication Data

Names: Fishman, Seth, author. | Bagley, Jessixa, illustrator.
Title: When I wake up / by Seth Fishman ; illustrated by Jessixa Bagley.
Description: First edition. | New York : Greenwillow Books, an Imprint of
    HarperCollins Publishers, [2021] | Audience: Ages 4–8. | Audience: Grades
    K–1. | Summary: "A young child contemplates four different paths their day
    may take"— Provided by publisher.
Identifiers: LCCN 2021025308 | ISBN 9780062455802 (hardcover)
Subjects: CYAC: Morning—Fiction. | Imagination—Fiction. | LCGFT:
    Picture books.
Classification: LCC PZ7.F5357 Wh 2021 | DDC [E]—dc23
LC record available at https://lccn.loc.gov/2021025308

21 22 23 24 25 RTLO 10 9 8 7 6 5 4 3 2 1
First Edition

 Greenwillow Books

For Caspian, go have your adventures. I'll be here.—S. F.

For Baxter—J. B.

The sky is dark when I wake.
Only the streetlights are on.

My mom says the sun is
always shining somewhere.

My dad says I should stay in my bed
until the clock shows 7:00 a.m.

But I do not want to stay in my bed.

put on my clothes

my own day.

Maybe I will do whatever I want to do.

I could make breakfast.

Or build a city.

Or take my scooter
down the alley.

Maybe I could even borrow
Mom's little shovel for the
garden.

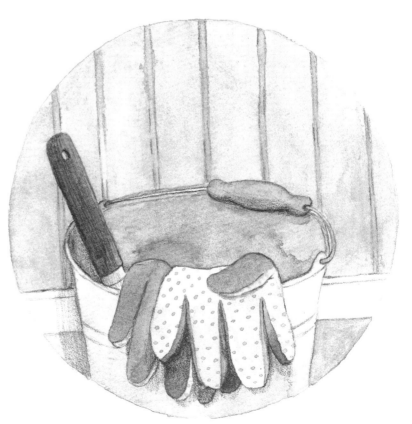

Mom likes bananas and Dad likes coffee, and I can pour my own milk.

My city is big enough for all my dragons and horses to live in.

I remember to zip my jacket
and to take one moment to
listen to the world.

I dig my own garden
right next to Mom's.

I'll clean up the mess later.

The horses in my city are better than the dragons.

I keep my foot far from the brake and roll down the hill forever and forever.

And save bugs from the cobwebs strung between the flowers.

Maybe I'll get marshmallows for breakfast too.

I tug on the horses' pink manes and launch them into the sky.

And when forever
is over, I'll climb
the gigantic
weeping willow.
I don't even
need a boost.

My mom says not
to kill spiders.
They help us
catch mosquitoes.
But I'm scared
of spiders.

I can sit in the closet
and eat the marshmallows
like Mom and Dad do
when they think
I'm not looking.

Shana, at school, has green hair.
Maisie has dark brown.

I'm scared of snakes too.
And of loud noises. And
of weird shadows.

The tree branches are pulled
down by all the kids who have
been here before me.

I don't even have to
brush my teeth yet.

My uncle's the one
who gave me the
horses.

The bark scrapes me as I climb. It hurts but climbing sometimes hurts.

I can always go back inside and find Mom if I'm scared.

I'm going to eat as many marshmallows as I can.

Maybe I'll call my uncle on Mom's phone and neigh like a horse.

Dad usually blows on my scrapes to make me feel better.

But this is my chance to explore alone, so I keep digging.

That was too many marshmallows.

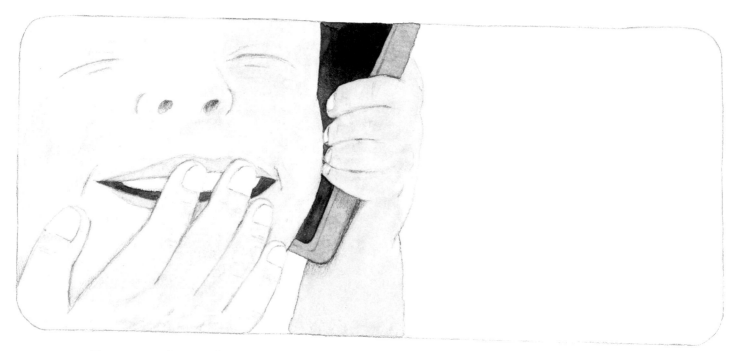

I wonder if my uncle will neigh right back at me.
Or if he'll do something else hilarious.

It's windy this high up in the tree,
but the breeze feels like Dad's breath on my cut.

Who knows what I'll find?

Of course,

that's just what I *could* do.

The clock doesn't say 7:00 a.m. yet.
But I leave my room anyway.

I don't think Mom and Dad will mind.

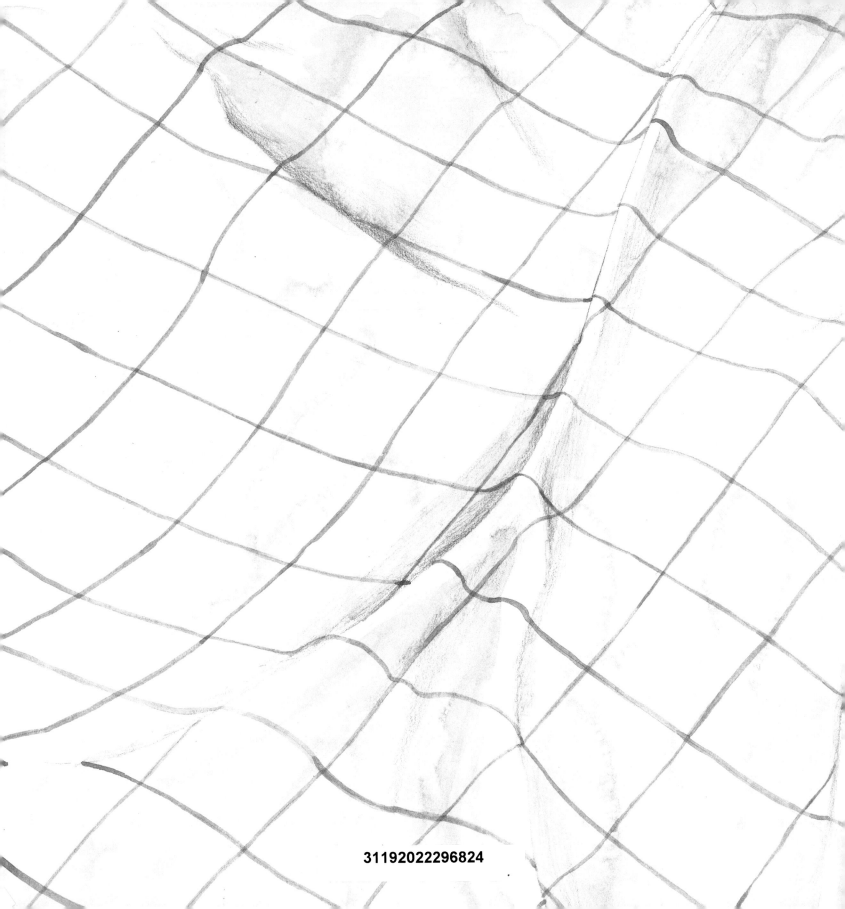

31192022296824